RollerCoaster Tycoon
TYCOON
Pick Your Path!

Sabotage!

For the four best friends a guy could ask for:
Jason, who unleashed my imagination;
Chad, who convinced me to ride my first
coaster; Marty, who drove me across the
country just to ride the Hangman; and Brock,
who keeps me from riding alone—S. B.

ISBN 0-439-49316-1

12 11 10 9 8 7 6 5 4 3 2 1   3 4 5 6 7 8/0

Printed in the U.S.A.   40

First Scholastic printing, January 2003

Pick Your Path!

By Shane Breaux

Cover illustration by Neil Stewart

SCHOLASTIC INC.

New York   Toronto   London   Auckland   Sydney
Mexico City   New Delhi   Hong Kong   Buenos Aires

He shoots! And he scores! Jason Jeffers reached up his arm to turn off his basketball alarm clock. It was 8 A.M. Even though it was the first day of summer vacation, Jason jumped out of bed and quickly got dressed.

"Morning, Dad," Jason said to his father as he ran into the kitchen.

"You're up early," his father said.

"I gotta go meet Max at Volcania!" Volcania was the theme park in New Carthage where they lived. Since Jason's dad was Volcania's park manager, Jason and his best friend, Max (Maximillian to all the adults they knew) spent every free minute hanging out there. Best of all, they never had to pay—or wait in long lines. They got maximum ride time every day!

"Son, I've got some bad news. Eruption is closed…"

"Aw, man!" Jason interrupted. "That's the most awesome ride at the park!"

"…and so is Velocity," Mr. Jeffers continued.

"Velocity's closed *again*? But you just got it running again last week."

"I know, but now there's some new problem with the ride."

Uh-oh, thought Jason. The rides at Volcania had been having a lot of "new problems" lately. And even though *he* never had to wait in them, he'd noticed that the lines for the rides looked much shorter than usual. Because of all the problems at the park since the season opened, the crowds just weren't coming like they used to.

"You'll figure it out, Dad." Jason tried to pump his dad up. "You solved other problems before. Volcania is the coolest, most excellent park in the world thanks to you!"

Mr. Jeffers shook his head. "It's not that easy. There's been so much trouble lately, the park owners have put me on notice. If I don't get things back on track, and soon, I'll lose my job."

"*What*?" Jason couldn't even imagine life without Volcania. "What would we do?"

"Well, Sandy Lagoon in California has made your old dad a job offer, so we won't starve," Mr. Jeffers tried to joke. "Don't worry, son. It'll all work out."

He patted Jason on the shoulder and went upstairs to finish getting ready for work.

"California!" Jason said to himself. "That means we'd have to move!" He didn't want to think about it. He rushed out of the house to meet Max.

The park was nearly empty when Jason got there. He flashed his season pass at the ticket taker and walked through the front gate. Then he headed for Eruption where Max was already waiting for him.

"Hey, man," Max said as he walked up. He nodded at the deserted coaster. "Closed for repairs."

"Yeah, I know," said Jason glumly, looking up at the ride. Eruption was an awesome-looking coaster, with a red steel track that shot straight up out of the mouth of the giant volcano, which was the center of the park.

Jason turned to his friend and explained his whole sorry situation: about the smaller crowds, the problems with the rides, and worst of all, California.

"California!" Max shouted. "That's totally lame."

"That's what my dad said. California."

"I can't take this!" Max said. "First Eruption and now California! Let's go ride the canoes at Lava Lake and try to enjoy our first day of summer."

There was usually a major line at Lava Lake. But today, they were able to hop right in a canoe, without having to pull their usual my-dad-runs-the-place card to cut in line. Max sat in front to paddle, and Jason got in the back to steer.

The lake bordered one side of the volcano. There were lava rocks jutting out of the water, creating a mini-obstacle course for canoes. It may have seemed dull to other die-hard coaster lovers, but Jason and Max loved it because just past the lava rock cliffs, the lake went underneath Inferno, the stand-up coaster. They could sit there forever watching the trains pass them by and listening to the people scream.

As they paddled around the cliffs, Jason felt cold water cover his toes. He looked down in surprise. The bottom of the canoe was filling up with water!

"Max! We're sinking!" he screamed.

"Hey, Jason, do you see that guy?" Max whispered.

"Dude, did you hear me? This canoe is going under!"

The water was now really pouring into the canoe. The two started paddling furiously to the side of the pond.

People in the canoes around them were sinking, too.

"Don't get my camera wet, Francine!" hollered a bald guy who was pulling a canoe with a large woman to shore.

"My brand new tube top is ruined!" wailed a girl who was dog-paddling in the water.

"Abandon ship!" Max cried. The canoe had filled with water so quickly, it was either jump or sink. They swam to dry land, climbed out, and began wringing out their T-shirts and shorts.

"This can't be good news for your dad," Max said to Jason.

"I know. California, here I come."

"No way, man," Max told his friend. "We're going to help him out."

"How can *we* help?"

"We'll investigate! Man, think about it. All the problems Volcania's been having, there's gotta be somebody behind it. Don't you see? Someone's trying to sabotage the park!" Max said excitedly.

Jason shook his head. "Max, you're crazy. I always knew one day you'd lose it, and finally you have."

"Well, what about that weird guy I just saw run out from the boat dock? He could have done this."

"I don't see anyone," Jason said, looking around.

"He's gone now, dude. Didn't you hear me say he *ran* from the boat dock! He may have been making a getaway!" Max said.

Just then a guy wearing Bermuda shorts and a Hawaiian shirt walked up them. "Hi, boys. I'm Larry Busby. You can call me Busby. I'm an investigative journalist, see." He pulled a notepad and a pencil out of his shirt pocket. "I'm working on a cover story for *Coasters Illustrated*. I've heard about the trouble here, and couldn't help but overhear your little conversation. So your father is the park manager, eh?"

Jason nodded, and Busy continued. "With my investigative experience and your knowledge of the park, the three of us could really crack this case!"

"What case? There hasn't been any trouble here. Well, a few mechanical problems, but it's no big deal. I'm sure there's an explanation for it." Jason tried to downplay all the trouble at the park.

"Well, I guess it *could* be just a coincidence that some of the rides have been malfunctioning this early in the season—and that attendance is lower than it's ever been. Or it *could* be that someone is trying to sabotage Volcania, just like your friend said! Do you want to work together or not?"

Jason and Max looked at each other. Was this guy for real? "Just a minute, sir," Jason said and walked off a ways with Max. "What do you think?"

"I don't know. It's his job to investigate stuff, so he could be a big help to us," Max answered.

Jason protested, "But what if his story makes things worse for Volcania? And my dad?"

Busby walked over and broke up their meeting

before Max could respond. "I don't mean to rush you boys, but time is ticking. The first thing you'll learn in investigation is that wasting time is like giving the criminals a 'Get Out of Jail Free' card. So. What'll it be?"

- Should Jason and Max work with Busby to crack the case? If so, turn to page 63.

- Or should they should tell Busby to take a hike and investigate on their own? If so, turn to page 39.

"Oh, no—wait!" Max shouted, "I see him! He's still at Lava River Rapids."

Jason looked in the direction his friend was pointing. "Where, Max?"

"Open your eyes, doofus. He's right *there*—by the ride exit."

"Oh, I see him now," Jason said. "Okay, let's get a little closer."

The boys walked toward The Creep, getting as close as they could without blowing their cover.

"What's he doing?" asked Max. The Creep was just standing there near the exit of River Rapids with his hands in his pockets, looking bored. The only thing he did was check his watch.

Suddenly, people on the rapids started shouting. "We're stranded! Help!"

Looking over at the Lava River Rapids ride, Jason saw that all the water was draining from the pool and gushing into Lava Lake. Some boats were carried away by the strong currents of the water and ended up in the lake. Without water to keep them afloat, others hit the concrete bottom of the pool.

"Max, do you see the river rapids?" Jason exclaimed. "All the water is draining out!"

"Yeah, I see. But, Jason, he's moving! The Creep is moving," Max whispered excitedly. "Let's go!" Max took off after their suspect.

But Jason was still watching the rafters float away or hit rock bottom. When he finally turned to join Max, he slammed right into the belly of a big guy. Jason looked up and said, "Excuse me," then ran to catch up with Max.

"Jason, I'm sure The Creep is responsible. This is the second time we've seen him at an accident scene.

"Look, he's on the phone again," Max observed. "Wonder what he's up to this time?"

They continued to follow him along the path as he walked across the park toward the park's volcano. The Creep stopped at the entrance of the Runaway Mine Train coaster. The ride's track twisted and turned through the volcano.

"Let's sit on a bench near the exit of the ride," Jason suggested. "We'll still be able to keep an eye on The Creep."

They waited, but nothing happened. The Creep put away his phone and just stood there. He scratched his nose, looked at the sun, and pulled some lint out of his coat pocket.

"Well, none of this is very suspicious, Max. Unless you want to debate whether he was scratching his nose or picking it."

"I know, but give it time," Max said. They sat there for a while until Max realized that it was too quiet. "Have you noticed that no one has gotten off the mine train ride since we've been sitting here? Is it running?"

Jason turned around in his seat to look at the ride. There was a trainful of people zigging and zagging along the track. "Yes, it's running. So what?"

"So that *means* it's been running for over ten minutes now—nonstop!" said Max.

Jason stood up and looked over at the ride entrance. There was a long line of angry-looking people waiting for their turn to ride. "You're right— he must have fiddled with the brakes! Boy, it's lucky for my dad this coaster only has one train. Think of the crash there'd be if two trains on the same track couldn't stop!"

"The Creep's moving again, Jason," Max said and got up to walk on.

Jason followed. He looked back at the mine train and saw the big-bellied guy he had run into earlier. That's strange, Jason thought. Is this guy following us?

They trailed The Creep closely as he weaved in and out of the crowds. Finally, he stopped at the go-cart track.

"Look at that, Max! All the go-carts are spinning out of control. And they all have flats!"

When they turned back, The Creep was gone— again.

"Well, at least we can be pretty sure of one thing," Jason said.

"What's that?"

"The Creep probably *is* involved and he *has* to be working with someone," Jason said, finally convinced. "There's no way he sabotaged the go-carts alone. We were watching him the whole time!"

As Jason and Max stood there watching the chaos, someone yelled, "Hey, you kids! I need to talk to you!" It was the guy with the big belly!

"Um, Max, I hate to tell you this, but I think we're in trouble," Jason said. "That guy's been watching us for a while. Both times a ride went down today, we were there!"

Max caught on to what Jason was saying. "He thinks *we're* the ones doing it!"

- **Should Jason and Max stay to talk to the big-bellied guy? If so, turn to page 106.**

- **Or should they run and hide from The Belly? If so, turn to page 16.**

The two boys both looked at Busby.

"Well, like Max said, it's a pretty good bet that the drill was used on the boats," said Busby.

"All right, fine," Jason said. "Let's follow up on the drill."

"Cool. But hold on to the pen," Max said, and Jason put it in his pocket.

"So let's look at the drill," Busby said, clapping his hands together. "Is there anything about it that would give us a lead?"

Max looked at it, turning it over in his hands. "Nope. It's just an old drill. It's so old, it looks like it could have been used by King Tut."

"Well, since the pen is a five-year gift, maybe the drill belongs to one of the employees," Busby said. "It could be that one of the maintenance workers has a beef against the park."

"Hey, you're right!" Jason said. "Let's go to the maintenance storage room where they keep all their stuff. We could talk to Sal. He's in charge of the tool room, so if this drill is missing he might know who last used it."

"You two are really good at this, you know?" Busby said.

Jason and Max grinned happily. The three of them left Lava Lake and headed toward the maintenance storage. They talked and laughed as they walked. Max was carrying the drill by his side—and Mr. Jeffers was heading their way!

- **Has Mr. Jeffers found out about Jason and Max's investigation? Turn to page 72 to find out.**

"If The Belly thinks *we're* the ones messing with the rides, that would really get my dad canned!" Jason said.

"Jason, what are you talking about, The Belly?"

"This guy has a huge gut."

"Whatever, dude. We haven't done anything wrong. There's nothing to worry about!" Max insisted.

"I know, but let's just get out of here," Jason pleaded and rushed away from the go-carts. Max reluctantly followed him. They ducked underneath the water slide, where they'd be safely hidden if The Belly followed them along the path.

"Dude, this is stupid!" Max complained. "We're totally innocent, and I'm sitting here getting dripped on by this waterslide."

"*Shh!* Let's just wait until he passes us. We need to get him off our trail so we can think."

"Well, you'd better think of something because by now we've really lost The Creep. Thanks a lot!" Max was getting pretty heated.

The boys crouched under the slide and waited for their follower to pass by. But he never did.

Instead, they heard a group of guys laughing and talking about all the problems at the park. They were all congratulating one another. Jason and Max stole a fast peek at the men. From their uniforms, Jason guessed they were all slide operators. And The Belly was with them!

"Look, Jason. There's the Belly! Who is he?"

"I don't know," Jason replied. "And what about the tall guy? He's not wearing a uniform, but he looks familiar. I think he might work here, too."

Their conversation was cut short when The Belly started talking. "I think I scared those two boys who were following you, Jimmy." He was talking to the tall man.

Jason and Max looked at each other. This was the guy they'd been following all morning—The Creep! He must have ditched the trench coat.

"Good thing, Rollo," Jimmy replied to The Belly, whose name was Rollo. "One of them is my boss's son!" So he did work at the park!

"You don't think they were on to you, do you, Jimmy?" one of the guys asked.

"I don't know. They were following pretty close.

Jason's never really met me, though, so I think we're safe," Jimmy replied. "I hope so. Operation Volcania Mania won't work if Jason finds out," Jimmy said.

Jason and Max looked at each other. "Operation Volcania Mania?" Jason whispered. "Why would the slide operators do anything like that?"

"Quiet. Listen, man," Max said.

"Since they got so close to blowing your cover," Rollo said, "maybe I should finish this, huh? I could do something like loosen the screws on one of the train wheels so it flies off and crashes!"

"No way, Rollo," Jimmy replied. "We don't want to hurt anyone. We just want that old fool Mr. Jeffers out of here."

"Who's he?" Rollo asked.

"He's our boss, you dummy," Jimmy said. "I explained all this to you when you agreed to help us out. He's the jerk who has refused to give us slide workers a raise all year! Well, this will show him to mess with us, right fellas?" All the operators nodded in agreement.

That was it. Jason and Max had heard it all. They left the slide operators quietly and hurried to find Mr. Jeffers. When they explained everything they had learned about the slide workers, Mr. Jeffers fired the whole group, and the trouble at Volcania stopped.

Jason and Max were the heroes of the park for exposing the saboteurs!

THE END

"Don't you trust your best friend, dude?" Max asked. "I have a feeling about this guy. He's totally involved—one way or another."

"All right, all right." Jason gave in. "Let's follow him."

They watched as The Creep crept around Hot Lava and headed toward the water rides.

"Investigating is almost as fun as riding," Max whispered.

"Nothing is as good as riding," Jason whispered back. "Wait a minute! Why am *I* whispering now?"

They were trailing their suspect by about ten feet when their big break came. A mother pushing a baby stroller was headed straight for The Creep. She was digging in her diaper bag and wasn't watching where she was going. To avoid having his shins rammed by a three-year-old's plastic limo, The Creep jumped to the side.

He avoided a full-on collision, but tripped on the stroller's front wheel at the last minute. Some papers dropped from his trench coat, but The Creep didn't notice. He kept right on going.

"Gold mine! Let's let him get away a bit and see what he left us," Max said.

"It's probably just his grocery list or a stupid love letter to Mrs. Creep." Jason still didn't think this guy was worth following. He was anxious to find out what trouble was happening over at the haunted house.

"We'll see," Max said. They scooped up the papers and hid behind the Lava River Rapids entrance to look at them.

"Keep an eye on The Creep while I look at this," Jason said.

"Don't worry, Jason. I won't lose him—I've got the eyesight of a rabbit."

"A rabbit?"

"Yeah. Rabbits have great vision. It's all the carrots they eat," Max said.

"Whatever, dude. Just keep your eyes on him," Jason said and turned to what they'd found. "It's just a couple of park maps. We give these out *free* to everyone who wants one. You know, like *park visitors* who come to enjoy the rides?"

"Let me see," Max said, taking the maps from Jason. "Hey, one of the maps is for I Scream Park. Isn't that Volcania's closest competitor?"

"Yeah. So what? He likes parks. So do we," Jason said. "They're just maps of...Hello! What's this?" Jason pointed to some markings on the Volcania map. "Look at this, Max. The haunted house *and* Lava Lake are circled."

"Ha! Those are the same sites that have had trouble today!" Max exclaimed. "I told you this guy was suspicious."

Max studied the Volcania map some more. He nudged Jason excitedly. "And look, the Lava River Rapids, the Mine Train, and lots of other rides are circled, too!"

"He's probably going to hit those places next!" Jason said and gave his friend a high five. "Max, you rule!"

"Yeah, I know," Max said modestly. "But come on. We've got to keep trailing him. We could catch him in the act of sabotaging a ride!"

Max looked up to check on The Creep but he

wasn't where he'd been standing a second ago. He was gone!

"Uh-oh," Max said. "I think I lost him."

"No, wait," Jason said. "I think I see him over there—"

- If you think Jason and Max have lost The Creep, turn to page 76.
- If you think Jason and Max find The Creep and keep trailing him, turn to page 9.

Jason and Max started to open their mouths, but Busby gripped the back of their necks roughly, shaking them. At the same time, Gene strode over to where they sat back-to-back on the floor and crouched down beside them.

"You don't want some innocent person to get hurt do you?" he whispered in a menacing voice. "Well, neither do I. But if you bring somebody else into this, I don't know what I might have to do."

There was another loud knock at the door, but this time Jason and Max didn't even think of trying to scream. Looking into Gene's crazed eyes, they could tell he meant every word.

They waited, still as statues, but whoever was at the door soon gave up. After several tense moments, Gene stood up and nodded at Busby.

Busby finished tying up the boys, making sure the knots were secure. Then he and Gene gathered the boxes and bags and headed for the door.

"Well, guys, I guess this is it," Gene said cheerfully. "I never meant for things to end *quite* this way, but I guess that's kind of your fault for nosing around. Oh, well."

He and Busby walked out, closing the door behind them. Then Gene stuck his head back inside.

"And boys, you can tell your dad not to even bother looking for me. Gene Patt doesn't exist—I made him up," "Gene" said with an impish grin. "Although since the rides won't be working come tomorrow morning, he won't really have a job to report to anyway, will he?"

With that parting line, he slammed the door shut.

Just like Gene predicted, all the rides malfunctioned, and Volcania never recovered. It closed immediately, and Mr. Jeffers lost his job.

Jason kept in touch with Max from California by e-mail.

THE END

Jason and Max both felt terrible for almost making Gene cry. How could they have thought Gene was involved with anything like sabotage?

Jason apologized. "Hey, Gene, we're really sorry, man. It's just that a lot of stuff has been going on, and my dad may get fired if things don't turn around here."

"Yeah, so we decided to try to figure it all out, and I guess we got carried away," Max added. "We know you'd never be involved in something like that. We're really sorry."

Gene looked at them for a moment. Then he nodded. "That's okay, guys. I understand," he said. "Hey, I've got a working model of Dragon Fly in the corner there. Do you want to check it out?" Just then the phone rang. "Let me just catch this."

While Gene was talking on the phone, Jason whispered to Max, "I can't believe we almost made him cry."

"No kidding, dude," Max said. "That was intense. There's no way he's involved."

"Yeah, we were *way* off. Let's get out of here and

call it a day. We can start again tomorrow," Jason suggested. "I'm hungry and tired, and I just wanna veg out and do nothing for a while. What you're supposed to do on summer vacation!"

"You said it, Jase!" Max replied.

When Gene got off the phone, Jason walked over to him and said, "Gene, we're really sorry about the mix-up. We hope we can still be friends. We'd love to take a look at the model of the Dragon Fly, but we're gonna take off, okay?"

"Sure, fellas. No hard feelings. I'll catch you later," Gene replied.

The boys left the basement and headed home. They had gotten all the way to the front gates when Max realized he'd forgotten his backpack in Gene's office.

"Aw, man. Do you mind if we run back real quick and get it?"

"Let's just hurry," Jason replied. "I'm starving."

They walked back to the offices again, headed down to the basement, and knocked on Gene's door. There was no answer, and the door was open slightly.

"Maybe he stepped out for a bite, too," Max guessed. "I'll just go in and get my bag."

But when they walked into the office, they saw that the place was a mess. Papers were scattered everywhere, Gene's chair was turned over, and the ride models were in pieces.

"What do you think happened in *here*?" Jason asked.

"Beats me," Max answered.

They searched around and found that all Gene's files had been cleaned out. And over at his desk, an error message was flashing on the computer: OPERATION SYSTEM SUCCESSFULLY DELETED.

"His entire hard drive has been wiped out!" Max exclaimed.

"Dude, this is major stuff," said Jason. "All the design plans for coasters in development are kept by the head engineer—Gene!"

With the assistance of the local police, the owners of Volcania launched a full-scale investigation, but Gene Patt had disappeared. Mr. Jeffers was able to keep his job, but it was a major setback for the park to lose the research and designs for so many awesome coasters.

Every now and then Jason and Max would wonder out loud about where Gene could have gone, but like everyone else, they had no clue. That is, not until the following season when Jason and Max saw a cover story in the April issue of *Coasters Illustrated.* The article, written by Larry Busby, was about a brand-new park that was opening, and all of its cutting-edge coasters.

"Jason, look! The guy who opened this new park kind of looks like Gene Patt," Max said, pointing to the photo next to the article.

"Yeah, but Gene Patt with dark hair and about thirty-five pounds lighter."

"Listen to this," Max said. He read the article out loud.

NEWEST ROLLERCOASTER TYCOON,
STEVE BATT, OPENS NEW PARK FEATURING
STATE-OF-THE-ART COASTERS

A sampling of the list of amazing rides

Steve Batt has built in record time are Joltage, B-52, and Dragon Fly—The Fire Flier. When asked about how he'd designed such a grand-scale park in a year's time, Batt had no comment.

THE END

Then Jason reconsidered. "Well, I guess it *does* make sense to go ahead and find out as much as we can about Gene while we're already here."

The boys walked around the entrance of I Scream until they found the door they were looking for. The door with the familiar sign that read: PARK PERSONNEL ONLY.

Jason went to knock on the door, but Max stopped him.

"Dude, what's the plan? What *exactly* are we going to say? I mean, I'd hate to get in trouble." Max was interrupted by a tall, skinny man approaching them. He was wearing a gray business suit, humming to himself.

"Follow my lead," Jason whispered to Max. "Excuse me, sir." The man stopped humming and turned around.

"Yes?" He said in a voice so deep it sounded like a joke. "Can I help you?"

"My name is, uh—" Jason stopped. Maybe he shouldn't give out their *real* names. The managers here didn't know that he was the son of the park manager at Volcania, and Jason wanted to keep that edge. "I'm Sherlock Jones, and um, this is my friend Watson."

"Oh, brother," Max said under his breath.

"We're working on a science project on the physics of roller coasters," Jason continued, "and we wondered if you could talk to us."

The man looked at them blankly.

"Well, actually we'd like to talk to some of your ride designers," Jason said.

"Yes! That would make our project *über*-impressive, sir," Max added. The man just stood there not saying a word.

Jason tried one more time. "Or maybe *you* are a designer and could talk to us." This guy was really starting to freak him out.

"Oh, gentlemen, I apologize for my rudeness. I'm Mr. Mackerel, the park manager here. I know very little about the physics of all this. I could introduce you to one of our designers, though."

"That would be great, Mr. Mackerel. Maybe we could even talk to Gene Patt."

"Yes, Gene Patt," Max piped up. "We've read in *Coasters Illustrated* he's one of the hottest designers in the country! Could we talk to him?"

"No, I'm afraid you can't," he said sharply. Jason and Max looked at each other.

Mr. Mackerel cleared his throat and started over. "No, you can't talk to him because Mr. Patt no longer works here. But we are fortunate to have another top designer who I'm sure will be more than happy to talk to you." Mr. Mackerel cleared his throat again.

Something is definitely going on here, Jason thought. But what? Jason and Max followed Mr. Mackerel into the office.

"Boys, this is Chip Muenster," Mr. Mackerel said. "He is the head designer at I Scream. Chip, these boys are doing a science project...."

Mr. Mackerel stopped suddenly and looked at them. "Isn't school out for the summer?" he asked.

"Um, yeah," Max said quickly. "But we're students at a summer science camp."

"Hmmm. I see," Mr. Mackerel said. Then he

nodded. "Well, Chip, they'd like to talk to you about physics and coasters. If you'll excuse me, gentlemen, I will leave you." He turned and was gone. Jason and Max breathed a sigh of relief.

Jason and Max didn't want to ask Chip about Gene Patt right away. That might be too obvious, so they just listened to what he had to say about coasters and gravity. It was pretty interesting— Chip really knew his stuff, but he talked forever! "Excuse me, Chip," Jason interrupted finally, "but where is the rest room?"

Chip told him, and Jason left him with Max. On his way to the rest room, he walked past Mr. Mackerel's office. He was talking on the phone.

"What's the update on Volcania?" Jason heard him say.

Jason stopped. He crept to the door to hear more. "How is everyone handling the chaos?" Mr. Mackerel was saying. He paused, then laughed. "Oh, great!"

Could Mr. Mackerel be involved? Carefully, Jason peeked into Mr. Mackerel's office. There was a trench coat hanging inside. It was the same color as The Creep's coat!

That didn't mean anything, of course, but any doubts that Jason had about Mr. Mackerel being The Creep went away when he heard him say, "Okay, Gene, I'll see you tonight. 'Bye." He hung up the phone and started whistling.

Jason ran back to Chip's office and said, "Thanks, Chip. You've given us some very good information for our project. We're sure to ace it. Come on, Max! We've gotta go. I've got to get home"—Jason winked at Max—"otherwise my dad will kill me!"

They ran out as quickly as they could. Jason explained everything to Max. When they got back to Volcania, he repeated the story to Mr. Jeffers. A full-scale investigation was launched, and the boys were right! Mr. Mackerel was working with Gene to wipe out their competitor, Volcania. It turned out that Mr. Mackerel had been under a lot of pressure to make I Scream the top park in the region, ahead of Volcania.

Around Volcania, Jason and Max were heroes! Even the owners of I Scream were grateful to Jason and Max for exposing the plot. They'd had no idea of Mr. Mackerel's scheme to sabotage Volcania and rewarded the two friends with free admission to I Scream! It was a supreme summer of rides and excitement!

THE END

One look at Max, and Jason knew his best friend felt the same way he did. Gene put on a good show, but he was definitely hiding something!

"Gene, we *did* do some checking up on you, but that was only after we found out some things that led us to you," Jason said. He gave Max a look that said, "play along."

"You wanna know how we found out about you working at I Scream?" Jason asked. "We were following this creepy guy after our canoe sank at Lava Lake, and he dropped some maps of Volcania and I Scream."

"On the Volcania map, all the rides that had been sabotaged were circled!" Max continued. "Do you expect us to believe that it was a coincidence?"

Gene didn't say anything.

"So who was the guy in the trench coat?" Jason demanded. Then he took a wild guess. "You know what we think? We think he's *your* partner!"

Max kept the pressure on. "Are we right, Gene?"

"Yes!" Gene yelled out without thinking. He gasped and covered his mouth with his hand.

"So it *was* you?" Jason whispered, shocked. Now that they knew the truth, he couldn't believe it.

Gene suddenly got furious. "All right, you nosy little nogoodniks! Lookie here. You should just mind your own business, and everything will be okay." Gene was scurrying around his office. He had totally lost it.

"What do I do now? Oh, what should I do now?" Gene asked himself as he paced around the room. "Get rid of them," he said softly. Then he charged Jason and Max shouting, "Get rid of them!"

- **Do Jason and Max stay and fight Gene Patt? If so, turn to page 43.**

- **Or do they try to reason with their friend? If so, turn to page 115.**

"No thanks!" the two friends said together.

"We can handle this ourselves, Busby," said Jason. "But good luck with your story."

"And good luck to you." Busby tipped his cap with a large hairy thumb and walked away.

"Okay, now that we got rid of that guy, we can get started," Jason said. "My gut is telling me to ask these folks at Lava Lake. You know, maybe they saw something."

"Are you deaf?" said Max, insulted. "*I* told you *I* saw a creepy guy run out of the boat dock, and…" Max suddenly stopped.

"What? What's wrong?" Jason asked.

"There he is!" Max whispered. "Over there!" Max pointed toward Hot Lava, the hyper coaster.

"That guy *does* look like a freak," Jason admitted. "Who wears a trench coat to an amusement park?"

"Nobody, that's who. Unless they're up to no good," said Max. "Let's trail him." They went around the boat pond and followed the creep to Hot Lava.

"Don't lose sight of him," Max whispered.

"What's with the whispering?" asked Jason.

"I don't want to blow our cover, doofus."

"Are you kidding me? We're at an amusement park! People are screaming all around us, and the guy is two rides away. He won't hear us," Jason said. Then he added, "Doofus."

"Whatever!" Max said loudly. "Let's just keep going before we lose him."

As they hurried past the Ferris wheel, they heard an urgent voice on one of the maintenance crew's walkie-talkies.

"Smiler, this is Grogan. You've got to come to the haunted house right away. And bring a couple of your guys with you, huh?" the voice said.

"Wait, Max," Jason said. "This sounds serious. Maybe something else is going on. Let me listen in for a second."

"But The Creep is getting away."

"Just keep an eye on him. Give me a minute; we won't be here long."

"But, Jason..."

"Shhh! I'm trying to hear!" Jason said. "Maybe *now* you should whisper."

Smiler, who was holding the walkie-talkie, responded to Grogan. "What's going on?"

Grogan explained, "I don't know, but all of a sudden, everyone's freaked—kids are crying and even the parents are running out of the house all upset. It's a mess! I need backup."

"We're on our way. Over and out." Smiler put the walkie-talkie back on his belt clip and ran toward the haunted house.

"This sounds like another hit!" Jason said excitedly. "Can you still see The Creep? What's he doing now?"

"He's on the phone."

"Well, if this haunted house thing is part of sabotaging Volcania, how could The Creep have done it? He was in our sight the whole time, right?" Jason asked Max.

"Yeah, but he could be giving orders on his cell phone."

"Well, what should we do?"

"Let's get closer to The Creep. That way we can hear what he's up to."

. . . .

"No way, man! We need to get to the haunted house pronto to see what's happening there," Jason said.

- If Jason and Max continue trailing The Creep, turn to page 20.

- If they head to the haunted house to investigate the new trouble, turn to page 68.

Gene charged right at Max and Jason! Luckily, there were two of them, and plus Gene wasn't exactly the most athletic guy.

Jason and Max lunged at Gene and wrestled him to the floor, kicking and swinging wildly. As they rolled around on the floor, they crashed into tables, taking down most of Gene's coaster models, papers, pens, computer discs, and other stuff.

At first, it seemed that Jason and Max would overtake Gene, but after a short while he gained the upper hand. As Jason bucked and kicked his legs trying to break free from Gene, he kicked open the door to the broom closet. In a sudden burst of strength, Gene pulled away from the boys and pushed them into the closet. Then, before they had a chance to recover, he slammed the door shut and wedged the back of a chair underneath the doorknob.

Jason and Max kicked and banged at the closet door, but it was no use. All they could do was watch through the door's small plate-glass window as Gene stuffed his bag with papers and CDs from the computer station. Then he ran out of the office.

"Help!" Jason yelled. "Somebody help us!"

"Dude, no one can hear you. We're locked inside a closet, in the basement," Max said. "We're going to be here a while, so we might as well sit down and wait it out."

An hour later, Jason and Max were trying to figure out how long they could go without food and water when suddenly someone opened the closet door. It was a guy from the cleaning crew.

"What in the world—" the man exclaimed, startled to see Jason and Max holed up in the broom closet. The boys jumped to their feet.

"Are we glad to see you!" Jason said. He grabbed Max by the arm and ran out of the office, leaving the man staring after them, bewildered.

The boys raced to tell Mr. Jeffers what had happened, but by then, Gene Patt was long gone. After an intense police investigation, they found that Gene had stolen years of exclusive research and ride-development plans done by the Volcania team. He'd sold the research to small parks for tons of money. A true computer whiz, he had also tapped into the park's financial accounts and made off with even more money. It was believed he'd moved to Europe where he'd sold the ride designs to major parks there—and gotten a new identity.

Volcania was in such bad financial shape, the owners of I Scream were able to buy the whole thing for much less than it was really worth. They renamed it You Scream. The only good thing was that Mr. Jeffers was kept on staff as the manager, and Jason and Max now had two parks to spend their time in—and twice the coasters to conquer!

THE END

"My dad was going to lose his job because of you two!" Jason argued.

"And you sank our boat! That is so not cool," Max added.

"We're sorry, kiddos."

"And stop calling us kiddos!" Jason yelled.

"Sorry," Peterson said quickly. "Just don't turn us in. I've got a wife and kids. What about them? If you turn us in, I won't be able to provide for them."

"Oh, you gotta be kidding me, Peterson. Don't take this the wrong way," Jason said, "but if you've worked here for sixty years, you must be at least seventy-five, which would mean your kids are probably grown-ups with their own families!"

"I've got three cats to feed! What about them?" Artie tried a new approach.

"Maybe Mr. Jeffers will go easy on you," said Max. "He's a good guy, right?"

"Yeah, great guy. If only he wasn't trying to get rid of us!" Peterson replied.

"Don't you want to retire? I think it would be fun. I wish I could retire from school," Jason said.

"Yeah, me too," Max added, "What's so great about running the Ferris wheel, anyway?"

Artie replied, "What'll I do with myself every day? I've been at this for so long, it's all I know."

"You said it, Artie," Peterson agreed. "I think I'd go stir crazy without having the haunted house to come to every morning."

"You'll find other things to do!" Jason said.

Peterson sighed. "I guess we'll have to. Come on, Artie. Let's go fess up to Jason's dad."

Jason and Max and Artie and Peterson left the house together and headed for Mr. Jeffers' office. Peterson came clean to Mr. Jeffers and told him everything.

"I can't believe you would do this to me, Petey!" Mr. Jeffers said. "After all these years. I knew you when the Ferris wheel was the scariest ride I'd get on."

"Yep. We're sorry," Artie said.

"Sorry," Peterson added.

Still, Mr. Jeffers had to fire them, especially after all the trouble they'd caused. New operators were hired for their rides. With the park's problems over, Volcania's success and popularity soared.

Jason and Max rode the newly fixed Eruption and other coasters every day that summer. And every once in a while, they ran into their old friends Artie and Peterson—just hanging out at the park.

THE END

"Busby's right," Jason said. "We gotta go tie him up or something, make sure he can't get away. *Then* we'll call the cops. Come on, Max. We can take him."

"Oh, all right. Let's go." Max wasn't all that excited about a rematch with Gene the Raving Lunatic. But there was no way he was going to let his best friend down.

The three headed back to Gene's office. There, they found him running around the room, frantically stuffing papers, discs, and CDs into a bag.

"I found these punks outside, Gene. They were really excited about solving this case. I thought you'd like them back down here," Busby said, grabbing each of them roughly by an arm.

Jason and Max looked at each other. What was going on?

"Good work, Busby," Gene answered. "After you tie them up, move these boxes of the ride developments and bank account information to the door. I'm almost done wiping out the information deck of the park's mainframe computer. Then we can go."

"What's going on?" Jason asked. "Busby, what are you doing?" Busby just tightened his grip on the boys and forced them to sit back-to-back on the floor. He started tying them up with the phone cord.

"You see, kids," Gene answered in a voice that did not sound like that of their old friend at all, "I'm getting paid a lot to steal company secrets. While my partner, Busby here, has been causing trouble with the rides to drive away the crowds," Gene said, "*I've* been collecting all of Volcania's coaster research and ride designs—which I'll sell, of course."

He laughed nastily. "They were so focused on fixing the problems Busby caused that they never even noticed what *I* was doing."

"You can't do this!" Jason cried.

Gene laughed. "I already have. And when I delete the mainframe, none of the coasters will function. The brakes won't stop, the launched coasters won't launch, and Volcania will be as dormant as the nonactive volcano in the park."

Just then there was a knock at the basement door. Everyone froze.

"Don't make a single sound," Gene hissed at the boys, his eyes wild. "Or else!"

- Do Jason and Max obey?
  If so, turn to page 24.
- Or do they scream their lungs out?
  Turn to page 102.

. . . .

"Busby is right, Max," Jason said. "I'm not ready to set her free just yet."

"Why not?" Max demanded. "What possible motive could she have?"

"That's what we have to find out. We should get her out of her office and search it," Busby suggested. "If she is guilty, the clues would definitely be in there. The trick will be to get her out of there."

"Max, she really seemed to like you," Jason said. "Why don't you offer to buy her lunch if she gives you the scoop on what it's like being a coaster designer? It could be a regular lunch date!" Jason laughed at Max.

"No way, man! I am *not* asking her to lunch," Max protested. "Why don't *you* do it?"

"I think she liked you a lot more than she liked me," Jason replied. "You gotta do it!"

"Oh, all right!" Max gave in. "But no one hears about this. Got it? I've got a rep to protect!"

"Our lips are sealed. Right, Busby?" Jason said.

"Yeah, you're a professional investigator now," Busby prodded Max.

Max returned to Ernestine's office. She was delighted to go out to lunch with him.

Jason and Busby waited outside for Max and Ernestine to leave the building. When they finally walked out the door and headed for the food court, Jason and Busby headed straight for Ernestine's office.

Once inside her office, Busby closed the door and looked at the clock on the wall. "It's one fifteen. We should try to be done in thirty minutes so we don't get caught," he said.

They frantically searched the whole office—digging in every drawer, box, and file they could find. They found nothing except coaster designs, printed e-mails, and porcelain frogs.

Jason looked at the clock. Fifteen minutes had already passed and they still had nothing. Jason was about to give up when he saw a porcelain frog about the size of a basketball near the door. The word JACKPOT was painted on it.

"Did you see that big frog, Busby?"

"Yeah, it's a cute doorstop," Busby answered

and continued quickly thumbing through the books on her shelves.

Jason went to the frog and picked it up. He turned it over in his hands. He noticed a hole in the bottom of the frog's right leg. "Jackpot!" he whispered to himself.

At about the same time, Max and Ernestine were at the Sushi Shop having their lunch date. She was the most charming old lady Max had ever met—he was actually having a good time! By the time they'd finished with their lunch, Max was convinced Ernestine was nothing but the sweet woman she appeared to be. He decided to come clean about their investigation. He knew she'd get a hoot out of it.

"And so that's why we came to your office!" Max laughed. "There's no survey—we were questioning you because we thought you might be a suspect! Isn't that hilarious?"

"Oh, that's pretty funny, all right," Ernestine said with a weak laugh. She picked up her napkin and started fanning herself with it. "Goodness, it's hot out here."

. . . .

"Yeah, Jason and Busby are in your office right now digging for 'evidence,'" Max continued, warming to his story. "What a waste of time. I told them—"

"*What*?" Ernestine screeched, cutting him off. She jumped up from the table and took off.

"Uh-oh," said Max. "Maybe I was wrong about her!" He hurried after Ernestine. Then he had an idea. While she raced to her office, Max ran to get Mr. Jeffers.

When Ernestine reached her own office, she flung the door open and saw Busby and Jason sitting on the floor. Her porcelain frog had been smashed, and its contents littered about the office. There was a small map of Volcania and some notes about possible ways to damage the canoes and Eruption!

"Well, Ernestine Bonds," Jason said. "We found enough evidence here to prove you were sabotaging Volcania!"

Ernestine turned to run, but she bumped right into Max and Mr. Jeffers, who were standing in the doorway.

"Ernestine, I can't believe it," Mr. Jeffers said in a heartbroken voice. "What on earth made you do this?"

"Money, that's what!" Ernestine said boldly, slamming her hand down onto the desktop.

"How would ruining our park bring you money?" Mr. Jeffers asked.

"Lots of parks out there pay lots of money for Volcania's research," she explained. "I'd set off a catastrophe to distract the engineer responsible for that ride. Whatever ride was damaged, that engineer would rush out to help fix it. That's when I'd sneak in to their offices and gather information on any developments they were working on.

"And it was working, too—until your do-gooder son and his nosy friends started poking around!" She looked at Jason, Max, and Busby with an evil glare.

And that was that. Volcania quickly regained its reputation as the greatest park in the country, and Jason and Max were featured in the article by Larry Busby in *Coasters Illustrated*. Their pictures were even on the cover. Ernestine Bonds was sent to jail and was never heard from again.

THE END

"I think we'd better walk," Max said. "I don't want to get trapped on an automatic ride."

"Me either," said Jason. "Let's go."

They gave each other a high five and crawled into the dark tunnel. Jason went in first, followed by Max.

"Man, I can hardly see a thing!" Max said.

"Feel around with your hands," Jason advised.

The mooing sound had morphed into a low laugh that never stopped for a breath. Both the darkness and the creepy sound surrounded them, making it impossible for them to figure out which direction it was coming from.

"This is totally crazy," Max said. "I can barely see you, and you're right in front of me." Max reached out with his hands to feel his way. Then he got an idea. He reached out to grab Jason's ankle and squeezed.

"Aaaaagh!" Jason screamed over the sounds of the house. "Something grabbed me!" Jason was yelling and scrabbling desperately to get away from whoever had grabbed his ankle. Then he heard his friend cracking up, and figured out it was Max.

They were finally out of the tunnel now, where the light was a little better and they could stand up. Jason shoved Max lightly for scaring him. "You bum!"

Laughing hysterically, Max stumbled into a wall. Only the wall was really a door. Max fell into the room, tripping over someone crouched by the door.

"Ow!"

That voice sounded familiar. "Who is that?" Jason demanded. "Peterson? What are you doing here? Is that *you* making those noises?"

Peterson ran the haunted house. He'd been in charge of the house since the park opened sixty years ago. He looked at Jason in the dim light with watery eyes and said, "Now! Why would I do…"

He stopped when he heard his voice amplified by the microphone he was holding. There was no denying it now! Peterson sighed and turned on a table lamp.

Max glared at the old man. "Peterson, you scared half the park away!"

Jason and Max were waiting for Peterson to

respond when they heard footsteps coming down the hall.

"Hey, Petey-boy!" someone called. "I drilled every last one of them boats! Sunk 'em, too." There was a gleeful laugh.

Any chance Peterson had of explaining this away was now gone with his partner's confession.

"Is that *Artie*?" Jason asked, outraged.

Peterson sighed. "Jason and Max are in here with me, Artie."

Artie was Peterson's best friend. An old-timer, too, he'd been running the Ferris wheel since the park first opened.

"What's going on? We were in one of those boats, Artie!" Jason was hurt. He and Max had known these two practically their whole lives.

"Sorry, kiddos," Peterson said. Peterson and Artie always called them kiddos.

"Yeah, sorry," Artie said.

"Just tell me why you did it," Jason demanded.

"Well, your father is forcing us to retire after this season," Peterson said.

"And we don't want to!" Artie added.

"No, we don't." said Peterson. "I've run this haunted house since Volcania opened sixty years ago, and I'm not going to give it up so easy!"

"And I've been running the Ferris wheel just as long. Why, we've given this park the best years of our lives!" Artie added.

"So you were going to get my dad fired by ruining the park? How would that help you?"

"Maybe the next guy would keep us on," said Peterson defensively.

Jason and Max looked at them doubtfully. The two men were pretty ancient, way past the age most people retired from working at the park. Jason knew the only reason they'd kept their jobs this long was that his dad was such a softie.

Peterson knew it, too. He slumped and said, "Mostly, I guess, we were just mad, and it felt good to stir up some dust.

"But we promise to stop. Maybe you could help out your old friends and not tell on us," Peterson pleaded.

"I don't know," Jason said.

"Hey, kiddos! It's Artie and Peterson, your pals," Artie said. "I gave you two rides on the Ferris wheel before you were brave enough for the coasters. Don't send us up the river, huh?"

- **Do Jason and Max turn Artie and Peterson in to Jason's dad? If so, turn to page 46.**

- **Or do give the old guys a break and let them go? If so, turn to page 81.**

"Well, he's going to do the story anyway," said Max. "We might as well make sure he gets it right."

"Plus, if we can figure this out, his story could really *help* my dad," Jason added. "We'd be heroes!"

"Right on, dude. Let's do it."

"Okay, Mr. Busby," Jason said. "We'll work with you."

Busby smiled, pleased. "Just call me Busby, boys. Now, what do you know so far?"

They explained everything about the sinking boats, the problems with Eruption and the other rides, and Max's sighting of the suspicious-looking guy in a trench coat. Busby was typing notes into his handheld computer.

"Whoa, Max. Look at his computer. I think we made the smart choice," Jason whispered.

"Do you see your suspect, Max?" Busby asked.

Max craned his neck and searched the distance. There was no sign of the guy anywhere. "Nope," he said, kicking the ground.

"No big deal. Right, Busby?" Jason tried to cheer Max up. "There are plenty of other things to look into, right?"

"Sure," Busby answered. "Tons."

There was a silence when no one spoke. Then Jason said, "Yeah. Like what do you think?"

"First, let's take a look at one of the canoes. Then, we should poke around the canoe dock where Max saw the guy. He may have left a clue or two," Busby said confidently.

"Yeah. That's what I thought, too," Jason said. "I just wanted to hear your idea first."

"Yeah, right, Jason," Max said. "Let's go look."

They pulled one of the sunken canoes out of the lake. After a quick inspection, Jason saw that there were holes drilled into the boat's bottom.

"How did the canoes float for so long before sinking?" he wondered. "We were paddling for a while before it started filling with water."

Busby leaned down to get a closer look. He noticed sticky pink stuff around the holes. "Bubble gum!" Busby said. "That's rich. They patched the holes with gum so that the boats would make it out into the lake before sinking!"

Max was glad they had accepted Busby's offer. He was already helping them find things!

They left the boat and walked around the lake to the dock. When they reached it, Jason asked, "So, buddy, where did you see the creep?"

"He was right over there," Max said. He walked to the opposite end of the dock near the holding area for the canoes. "He crawled out of these weeds."

"All right, let's look around, boys," Busby said. The weeds went up to their knees, so Jason and Max dropped to the ground to feel around for anything their suspect might have left behind.

"Ooh, gross!" Jason yelled.

"What?" Max asked.

"Someone lost their lunch, and I found it!" Jason yelled. He ran to the lake to rinse his hands. Busby howled with laughter as he dug around the weeds, too.

"Isn't this fun!" Busby exclaimed.

Jason didn't see what was so much fun about dipping his hand in puke, but he went back to work.

"Whoa! Stop everything, dudes. Look what I found," Max said as he lifted a power drill from the ground. "This could have made the holes in the boats, right?"

"That makes sense to me, Max," Busby agreed.

"Ha ha! See? I told you. The guy was here!"

"Good work, Max," Jason said.

Busby found something, too. "Well, here is an ink pen—a *nice* ink pen, but that doesn't help us." Busby started to toss it, but Jason stopped him.

"Wait a second, let me see that." Busby handed the pen to Jason.

"Hey, these pens are given to people after they've worked at Volcania for five years," said Jason. "My dad has one. His has his initials engraved on it. And so does this one! This pen belongs to EXB."

"Yeah, so what?" Max demanded. "The drill's a

much better lead than a stupid old pen. We should start with that."

Busby took the pen again and peered at it closely. "Hmmm. Very curious, this pen." He recorded some information into his computer.

"Think we should follow up on it?" Jason asked, ignoring Max.

"Well, clearly," Max tried again, "we need to try to find the owner of the drill. Obviously, no one made any holes in the boats with an ink pen!"

"Well, clearly," Jason responded with annoyance, "there's the possibility the pen and the drill belong to the *same person*. And since we know the person's initials, we should start there!"

- If the trio follows the pen lead and searches for EXB, turn to page 110.

- If they follow the drill lead and search for its owner, turn to page 14.

"But our suspect is getting away!" Max pleaded with Jason as he ran after him. They were heading for the haunted house.

"Max, a guy in a trench coat does not make a suspect. It makes a freak-a-zoid who is afraid of getting too much sun. Besides, it's not like you actually saw the guy doing anything wrong, right?"

"Yeah, but..." Max stopped. They had reached Lava Lite, the kiddie section where the haunted house was located. All around, children were wailing and being comforted by their parents. "Hey, I wonder what happened here."

"Whatever it was, it must have been major— look at all those kids crying!" Jason exclaimed.

"Dude, you're not kidding! There's even a barricade around the house. Whatever happened was so major they shut the whole place down!" Max replied.

Then they heard a blood-curdling sound. "Whoa! What *is* that?" Jason yelled over the sound of wolves yowling, people screaming, and hawks screeching.

"I don't know. Is it coming from the house?" Max yelled back.

"What?" Jason couldn't hear a thing over the shrieking.

The noise was getting louder and louder. People were running away from the haunted house as fast as they could.

"Leave the baby's diaper bag, Peggy!" a frightened mother yelled. "Let's just get out of here!" Holding her baby in her arms, she grabbed Peggy's hand and ran.

Even the workers freaked out and ran. An employee who operated the slide next to the haunted house was in such a hurry, he actually shoved a five-year-old kid out of his way!

"I think the noise is coming from the house!" Max tried again.

"I can't hear what you're saying, dude, but I think the noise is coming from the house!" Jason yelled.

Then the noise stopped. It was quiet again. Every last person in Lava Lite was gone.

"This is not good for business," Max said in a quavering voice, trying to stay cool.

"Well, maybe we should go in the house and check it out?" Jason suggested without much enthusiasm. He was pretty freaked out himself.

"Man, that noise was brutally bad. Not to mention creepy!" Max protested. "I don't think we want to go in there."

"We don't have much choice, Max." Jason tried to gather some courage. "I'm not going to let some stupid kiddie spook house move me to California."

Without waiting for a response, Jason marched up to the house and tried the door. "Locked," he said. Then he froze. A new sound was coming from the house. This one was a low-pitched rumble.

"Let's try the window," Jason suggested. He walked over to the window and tried it. "It's open. Come on, chicken," Jason said, disappearing inside the dark house.

Max followed him inside.

"Look!" said Jason, pointing at a train. "I rode this once when I was little," Jason said. "The train takes you through each room, then it stops and a light comes up and shows you a horrific scene. It's kind of scary—for little kids."

"Well then, I say we hop on it and check out the house," Max said.

"We can reach more places by walking. Plus, I wouldn't be caught dead on this dumb old ride," Jason said.

The words were barely out of his mouth when the scariest laugh either of them had ever heard echoed through the house.

- **Do Jason and Max take the train to explore the house? If so, turn to page 95.**

- **Or do they explore the dark house on foot? If so, turn to page 58.**

Busby wandered off from the boys so Mr. Jeffers wouldn't know he was with them.

"Hiya, Dad!" Jason said brightly.

"Well, hi, boys," Mr. Jeffers replied. "Where are you headed?"

"Oh! Uh. Hmm," Jason struggled to find a lie. He didn't think his dad would like the idea of him and Max investigating the trouble. But before he could come up with an answer, Mr. Jeffers interrupted him.

"Hey, Max, where did you get that drill?" Mr. Jeffers asked abruptly.

"Oh, we found it," Max said. "It was near Lava Lake."

"Well, I'm going to take it with me," Mr. Jeffers said in a tight voice. "This can be very dangerous, and I'm glad you found it." Max handed him the drill reluctantly, and Mr. Jeffers practically snatched it out of his hands.

"Max, I need to borrow Jason for a little while," Mr. Jeffers continued. "He'll catch up with you later."

All Jason could do was look at Max before his

dad led him toward his office. From the way his dad was acting, Jason just knew that he was busted for sneaking around the park all day. If Max had just hidden the drill, this wouldn't have happened!

When they reached the office, Jason plopped down on his dad's sofa. Mr. Jeffers closed the door. "I'd rather you hear this from me than from anyone else. I never should have started this, but I did. Now it's getting to be too much to handle," Mr. Jeffers said.

"Dad, what are you talking about?" Jason asked. Maybe he wasn't in trouble after all.

"It's my drill, son."

"What!" Jason said loudly.

"I'm the one who drilled the holes in the canoes. I dismantled the trains on Eruption. I did it all."

Jason couldn't believe what he was hearing. "That doesn't make any sense. Why in the world would you do that?"

"Here's the thing. Every six months for the past couple of years, I've applied for a promotion. I want to be a full partner in the business. You know, part owner. And they always tell me the same thing. 'Not right now. You're a great manager, Jeffers.'"

"So you sabotaged the park?" Jason asked, confused. "How would destroying your own park help you? Did you just want revenge?"

"No, not revenge. My plan was that I'd cause a few problems that seemed impossible to fix, then I'd fix them. They'd see how great I was, and they would promote me."

"*You* would solve the problems that *you* were causing?" Jason was getting a headache.

"Yes, but all they'd know was that I solved the problems, and I'd be the hero!" Mr. Jeffers said. "It really seemed like a good idea before I started the whole mess. Now I realize what a crazy idea it was. I can't stay on here. I'm going to have to come clean and quit the park."

And he did. Mr. Jeffers told his bosses the whole story and quit the park. It was the hardest thing he'd ever done, but he knew it was the right thing.

With his reputation as a park manager destroyed, there was no way he'd get the job in California now, or at any other park for that matter.

Mr. Jeffers thought about what he could do next. Then it hit him. As bad as he felt for the trouble he'd caused at Volcania, he remembered he was pretty good at it. He could open his own practical-joke and gag-gift shop! That way he could play pranks all day long and help other people play them, too—and he wouldn't get in trouble for it!

Jason and Max were heartbroken that they didn't have their run of Volcania anymore. But at least their park passes were good for the rest of the season!

THE END

"Let's check all the rides circled on the map! He might have gone ahead to one of them," Jason suggested.

"Okay," said Max.

They checked all the sites but couldn't find The Creep anywhere. They finally gave up.

"He's gone," Max said.

"What about your 'rabbit' eyesight?" Jason said sarcastically.

"I thought I had him, but he must have slipped away while *I* was figuring out the clues on the map."

"You let our one and only lead get away!" Jason couldn't believe it. "Now what?" Jason scratched his chin and thought for a while. He was stuck. "Maybe we should have used that reporter's help."

"Yeah, I guess so," Max said. "What else can we do?" He looked down at the two maps in his hand. Growling in frustration, he crumpled them up and tossed them over his shoulder, hitting Jason in the head.

"That's it!" Jason shouted.

"What? What's it?"

"Here's our other lead," Jason said, picking up the crumpled map of I Scream. "We should investigate at I Scream and see what turns up."

"Yeah! Maybe weirdo things have been happening there, too."

"Or maybe," Jason added, "The Creep's on his way there right now!"

The boys left Volcania and headed straight for I Scream. As they approached the park, they could see the beautiful steel structures reaching into the sky. All those coasters in one place was enough to make them crazy!

"Don't we have time for just one ride?" Max begged.

Jason shook his head. "Uh-uh, The lines here are way too long."

"But I have never, in *all* my days on earth, been to a park and *not* ridden. That would be like going to the movies and leaving after the previews—before the actual movie starts. It's just not right!"

"Calm down there, Hyper Henry. We're here to save Volcania. California and all that, remember?"

"You're right," Max gave in.

The boys paid for their admission and entered the park. They were looking at and listening closely to everything. Anything could be a clue. And they kept their eyes peeled for The Creep.

As they walked past the lockers and rest rooms, Jason stopped and pointed. "Look, Max. Do you see the pictures of the employees of the month?"

"Yeah. A bunch of guys who actually get paid to spend the day at an amusement park. I'm jealous. What about them?"

"Do you recognize October's Employee of the Month?"

Max stepped closer to the photo. "Hey, it's Gene, Gene the Designin' Machine! I didn't know Gene Patt worked here!"

"Me either. And according to his plaque, he was Employee of the Month eight times in the last few years including last October. Which means he worked here until the end of last season," said Jason.

"My dad says Gene is the best coaster designer he's ever met, and he's not much older than we are," Jason continued.

"I believe it," said Max. " That guy's a genius! I love the ride he's working on for next season—that flying coaster is going to rock so hard!"

"That's true," Jason said. "In fact, it's almost too good to *be* true."

"What do you mean?"

"Well, think about it—if he's so good, why did this park let him go? Don't you find it strange that as soon as he starts working at Volcania, the park starts falling apart?"

"Wait a minute. You think *Gene's* involved in the trouble?" Max asked.

"Maybe. Wouldn't it take someone who really knew how the rides worked to cause the kind of trouble that's been happening?" Jason said. "I think we should dig up all the dirt we can on Gene Patt."

"Right, Sherlock, but how?"

"We'll just talk to him. We'll pretend that nothing's up, hang out with him like normal, and see if he lets any information slip."

"I don't know, Jason," said Max. "I think we should start by talking to the people around here and get the 411 on why he left."

"No. Let's get down to business, dude. We'll get the skinny straight from the Machine himself. We can be smooth enough not to let on about what we're really doing. He'll never suspect a thing!"

- **What should Jason and Max do? Should they continue snooping around I Scream for information about Gene Patt? If so, turn to page 31.**

- **Or should they head back to Volcania to talk to Gene? If so, turn to page 86.**

"I gotta tell you, Jason," Peterson said, "if I get fired, I lose my pension. I can't afford that!"

"Yeah, kiddos. Just let us retire nice and quiet-like. We won't cause any more trouble," Artie promised.

Jason and Max looked at each other and sighed. They both knew what they would do.

"Okay, Peterson," Jason said. "Just cut it out, all right? You almost sent me off to California!"

"Hey, thanks kiddos," Artie said, "I guess I'd better get back to the wheel. My shift is about to start." He was gone.

"Thanks, boys," Peterson said. "Hey listen, you want to have a turn at making scary noises with this microphone? It makes your voice sound really creepy."

"I don't think we should," Jason said.

"Why not, dude? It'll be awesome," said Max. "Plus the ride is closed. No one's even around."

"It's a lot of fun, even for an old coot like me," Peterson put in.

"All right," Jason said. He picked up the mike

and started cackling with laughter into it. His voice sounded sinister through the speakers. It was great!

Peterson left Jason and Max as they took turns spooking each other and trying to create the creepiest voice. He met up with Artie at the Ferris wheel. "Hey Artie! Take a break and come with me. I've got a brilliant idea."

The two men made their way to Mr. Jeffers's office at the front of the park. They walked into his office, and Peterson said, "Mr. Jeffers, I just went back to the haunted house because I forgot my lunch pail. When I got there, I heard such a racket that I rushed in to see what was going on. And there they were—whooping and hollering and making the worst noises you ever heard!"

"Petey-boy, you're a genius," Artie said under his breath as he figured out his friend's plan.

"Who, Peterson? What are you talking about?" Mr. Jeffers asked.

"Jason and Max," said Peterson. "They're the ones who've been causing all the racket at the haunted house all day!"

"What?! Are they there now?"

"Well, sir, they're still there now, probably going to town with their antics," Peterson said.

Artie chimed in, "If you ask me, they're the ones behind all the shenanigans."

"Let's go!" Mr. Jeffers said.

The three men rushed to the haunted house. Sure enough, there were Jason and Max howling and screeching into the microphone.

"Jason Gregory Jeffers! You stop that foolishness right now!" Mr. Jeffers was shocked and angry that his own son was responsible for scaring so many children.

"But Dad, Mr. Peterson told us we could—" Jason tried to explain what was going on, but Mr. Jeffers wouldn't listen.

"I am very disappointed in both of you," Mr. Jeffers said. "I'm taking away your park privileges for the rest of the summer—at least. And what about the boats? I assume you two were responsible for that, too?"

"No! Dad, please just listen to me—" Jason tried again, but Mr. Jeffers cut him off.

"People could have been seriously hurt, Jason. I don't think it's such a good idea for you and Max to hang around each other anymore. We'll discuss this again at the end of the summer."

Then Mr. Jeffers turned to Peterson and Artie. "Gentlemen, I'll appreciate your not telling anyone about this. I don't think my boss would like the idea of my son and his friend causing such a scare here today.

"And I'll talk to the boss about your retirement, too. You can stay on—I'll make sure of it."

Peterson and Artie assured Mr. Jeffers that they were extremely grateful and would never tell anyone about Jason and Max.

The weirdness at Volcania stopped, and Mr. Jeffers kept his job. Peterson and Artie continued to run their rides. And Jason and Max had a miserable coaster-less summer.

"There's always next year," Max wrote to Jason in an e-mail, their only form of communication now that they were both grounded for the summer.

"Yeah. Well, at least I'm not stuck in California," Jason wrote back. " 'Talk' to you tomorrow."

He signed off and gazed out his window, where he could see Volcania's tallest coasters against the skyline. He wouldn't be riding any coasters for a while, but at least he could enjoy the view!

THE END

Max gave in. "I guess you're right. Maybe we *can* get something out of Gene. Now are you sure we can't sneak in one little ride?"

"You're killing me, Max! Killing me. Let's go."

They returned to Volcania and headed straight for Gene's office. It was in the basement of the building where the design and research teams' offices were located. Most people would hate being in the basement, but Gene's office was pretty cool. Gene liked it because he didn't like being disturbed—it was away from everyone else and totally private. Jason and Max liked hanging out there because it had its own entrance, and it was huge, with lots of working models of roller coasters the boys could play with. There was even a sofa and easy chairs, a TV, and a mini-fridge!

When they arrived, it was late and Volcania was closed. The park was deserted except for the maintenance crews doing their final ride checks for the day. But Jason and Max knew Gene would still be working; he always worked late.

Max dropped his backpack and plopped down on the sofa. "What's up, Gene?"

"Hey, Gene, my man! How goes it?" Jason tried his best to act natural.

"It goes great, fellas." Gene replied in his nasally voice. He pushed up his glasses. "How goes it with you?"

"Great, Gene, just great! I love summer vacation!" Jason replied enthusiastically. "What are you working on?"

"I've almost got all the kinks worked out of the new flying coaster for next season. I've just got to slow the train down about twelve miles per hour before the final helix and double dip, and it'll be set!"

"That coaster is gonna be so cool!" Max said. "I can't wait to ride it."

"Yeah, Volcania is majorly lucky to have you here," Jason added.

"Well…" Gene blushed, embarrassed by the compliments. "I can show you the latest screen demo of what I am calling Dragon Fly—The Fire Flier. Take a look."

The three took a virtual ride of the Dragon Fly on Gene's computer screen. It really was going to be a beautiful ride. There were two loops and two heart-line twists. It was designed to fly around Eruption, then go in and out of the volcano before ending over the water of Lava Lake.

At the end of the demo, Gene said, "Great, right fellas? And I'll tell ya what. I'll see to it that you're given the first ride when it gets built. How's that?"

"Rock on, Gene." Jason nodded. Then he glanced at Max and said, "Sooo, Gene, where did you build these smoking coasters before you came here?"

"I was at I Scream until last October," Gene replied.

Max played dumb. "Really? So what brought you here?"

"Well, the pay is better here. And Mr. Jeffers is such a nice guy to work for. He really appreciates his staff, much more than my old boss did at I Scream."

Max and Jason glanced at each other. What about his multiple awards for Employee of the Month?

"Plus, Volcania has much better coasters, right? It's cool working at the number-one park in the region," Gene finished.

Sounded good to Max. He looked at his friend doubtfully, but Jason pressed on.

"Gene, what do you think about all the stuff going on here?"

"Stuff? What stuff?" Gene turned away and started organizing his desk, which was already perfectly neat.

"My dad told us about the trouble the park's in. Plus we were canoeing when all the boats at Lava Lake sank!"

"Yeah, Gene. Tell us what you know," Jason said.

"Hey, fellas, your dad asked us not to talk about it with anyone."

Max got serious, "Look, you worked at I Scream before, and we know that you were awarded Employee of the Month there for like ten months, so what's this stuff about their not appreciating you? What are you lying about?"

"What do you mean? You've been checking up

on me? Come on, guys. I thought we were pals." Gene's eyes actually started to tear up. "This is the best place I've ever worked. That's why I came here. Volcania has the most funding for developing new rides than any other park I know of. I couldn't have developed a ride like the Dragon Fly at I Scream.

"Boys, I hate what's happening here, but Mr. Jeffers is a great guy. He'll figure it out. Now, if you'll excuse me, I need to do some work. Please go." Gene stood up, walked to the water cooler, and filled a paper cup with water.

- **Do Jason and Max believe Gene's story? If so, turn to page 26.**
- **Or do they think he's guilty? If so, turn to page 37.**

"No way, man," Jason said. "I'm not crazy enough to go back down there. This is definitely one for the cops."

Busby backed down, though they could tell he was just itching to burst into the office and save the day. "All right boys, here's my cell phone to call the police. We should stay here, though, in case he tries to leave the building. We'll get him if he does."

Jason dialed the police. He also called his dad, but Mr. Jeffers didn't answer. Jason left a message on his voice mail.

He hung up the phone and sat down with Max and Busby to wait for help when Gene rushed out of the basement. He was loaded down with bags stuffed with files, discs, and CDs.

Gene stopped when he saw Jason and Max waiting for him. "You two still here?" he snarled nastily.

His lip curled and he looked like he was about to attack them again. But then he noticed Busby with the boys and his shoulders slumped. He knew he couldn't take on all three of them. He dropped his bags and took off running into the park. The boys chased after him, and Busby followed.

"Look! He's heading toward Lava Lake!" Max yelled as he ran.

Gene jumped into the water and ran back out at the opposite end. They followed him. It was hard running in wet clothes, and Busby was really trailing behind.

"He's going to Lava Lite!" Jason said. By this time, the maintenance workers saw Gene running through the park, and they picked up the chase.

They all followed him through the center of the park, past Eruption and the huge volcano it erupted from, straight into Lava Lite, the kiddie section. Gene dove through a window of the Crooked House. Jason, Max, Busby, and six workers followed Gene through the window. They all ran through the hallways of the house.

Gene escaped through a rear window and left Lava Lite. He ran to the log-flume ride, and jumped from boat to boat in the station. "I'm going after him," Jason said, pulling ahead of Max and the others in a sudden burst of speed.

He followed Gene to the log-flumes, hopping from boat to boat to stay on his trail. Able to balance himself in the rocking boats better than Gene, Jason caught up with him quickly. He grabbed Gene's shirt. When Gene tried to shove Jason off, they both lost their balance. They fell out of the flume and into the water.

"I can't swim! Help!" Gene yelled.

Jason walked over to Gene (the water was only chest-high) and held the flailing man up so that he wouldn't drown.

He held on to Gene until they reached land. Busby, Max, the maintenance crew, and Mr. Jeffers were there waiting to help pull them from the water and keep an eye on Gene until the police arrived.

Jason and Max took turns explaining how they'd figured everything out.

"Jason, Max," Mr. Jeffers said. "I can't tell you how impressed I am with both of you. I never would have suspected Gene Patt would do this—he had us all fooled. If not for you, we might not have found out what he was up to until it was too late!"

Mr. Jeffers couldn't have been more proud of Jason and Max. To celebrate, he took them both to Sandy Lagoon in California. They spent three whole days riding all the cool coasters.

"I guess this would have been your life if Gene had pulled off his scheme," Max said to Jason.

"I guess so," Jason answered, "but as awesome as these rides are, nothing beats home!"

THE END

"Did you hear that creepy laughing?" Jason asked.

"Yes!"

"Maybe we should just hop on the train—it *is* too dark to go on foot." Jason said shakily.

Max nodded, relieved.

"Grab a seat, Max, and I'll try to get it running and hop on before the train leaves the station."

Max sat alone in the front car while Jason went to the control box and fumbled around until he found the right switches. He said, "All clear," and pushed the Go button. The train rumbled to life and slowly pulled out of the loading dock. Jason easily slipped into the seat next to Max. "Keep your eyes peeled for anything weird."

The frightening sounds continued, but now there was the added sound of a siren.

"Whoa!" Max said. "What's with the sirens?"

The train made a sharp turn to the left and stopped suddenly. Lights came on to their right and a scene of a ghost flying through trees was revealed.

"That is so dumb," Jason said.

"Yeah. Oooh, I'm so scared!" Max said sarcatically.

The low moaning noises grew louder, and the horrible screeching sound they'd heard when they first arrived at the house took over.

Jason and Max sat speechless. Now they really *were* scared, not that they would ever admit it. The train continued on its usual route: go a ways, make a sharp turn, stop suddenly, then light up on a lame scene of horror. Nothing too frightening—if you didn't count the creepy sounds echoing throughout the house.

"Man, those noises are killing me!" Max yelled, covering his ears.

The train made its final stop at the swamp creature's lagoon before rolling back into the station. Just as the train stopped in the station, Mr. Jeffers jumped in front of the train wearing an angry glare on his face.

"Aaaaagh!" both boys screamed, startled. Mr. Jeffers looked more furious than Jason or Max had ever seen him. He pressed a button on a remote-

control device he was holding. The siren stopped but the other weirdo noises continued.

"It's okay, Dan. No one broke into the house. I found a squirrel, and he must have tripped the alarm," Mr. Jeffers lied into his walkie-talkie. Then he turned to the boys, shaking his head.

"I am really disappointed in the two of you. I can't believe you're in here playing around."

"No, Dad, we're not. You see…Um…" Jason was really nervous. "I don't want to move to California, and we thought we could help you find the person who was sabotaging the park."

"Sabotage?" Mr. Jeffers sounded confused.

"You know, all the bad stuff that's been going on around here."

"And we saw a guy in a trench coat, but we lost his trail, so we came here to see what we could find," Max said, then added, "Sir."

Mr. Jeffers chuckled, then stopped himself. "Let's go outside. I can't talk with all this racket!"

They walked out the front door and sat on a bench in the shade. "I appreciate your wanting to help me out with this, but you should have stayed out of it. I'd lose my job a lot quicker if they found out you were trespassing in a closed area of the park. You set off the alarms here!"

"Sorry, Dad. We didn't know that the siren noise was an alarm. We thought it was part of the spooky noises that frightened all the guests away from the haunted house today."

"Speaking of those noises," said Mr. Jeffers, "they're not part of some big mystery that needs to be solved."

"They're not?" asked Jason.

"No. The haunted house team tried out a new sound track that turned out to be too frightening. There's a malfunction, and we can't turn it off."

"And you'll be happy to know that the other problems we've been having have been solved as well," Mr. Jeffers continued. "There was no plot of sabotage—just bad luck. Eruption and a couple of the other coasters just have some mechanical kinks that we have to work out. And once we do, things will function like normal. It's as simple as that."

"What about the boats?" Max asked.

"Well, you were on the right track about that one. That *was* done by an employee, someone I had to fire last week. He was angry with me, and he tried to get revenge by drilling holes in the bottoms of those boats. But we caught him trying to sneak out of the park about half an hour ago, so it's being taken care of."

"So no California?" Jason asked.

"No California," Mr. Jeffers said. "You two can't just run around like you own the place! I'm going to tell the staff that from now on, you and Max are no longer allowed to cut in lines. You'll have to wait like everyone else. And you can start waiting right now—Eruption is running again."

Feeling sheepish, Jason and Max walked over to Eruption for their first ride of the summer.

"Obviously, we're not out to be private investigators," said Max. "Guess we should stick to riding coasters, huh, Jase?"

"You said it!" said Jason as the two boys took their place in the long line.

THE END

"It was a nice try, Jason. She *could* have been part of the plot to bring down Volcania," Max teased, "but she was too busy designing a new roller coaster for six-year-olds called LadyBug!" Max was cracking himself up.

"Come on! How was I supposed to know that EXB was a grandmother? She could have been someone extremely dangerous." Jason tried to defend himself.

"Yeah, beware of Ernestine Bonds and her porcelain frogs!" Max was doubled over laughing.

"Let's check out the drill." Busby changed the subject to spare Jason. "Is there anything about it that could link it to its owner?"

Max looked at it, turning it over in his hands. "Nope. It's just an old drill. It's so old, it looks like it could have been used by King Tut."

"Well, since the pen is a five-year gift, maybe the drill belongs to one of the employees, too," Busby said. "It could be that one of the maintenance workers has a beef against the park."

"Hey, you're right!" Jason said, "Let's go to

the maintenance storage room where they keep all their stuff. I bet we could find out some good info there."

The three headed off to the maintenance storage. They talked and laughed as they walked. Max was carrying the drill by his side—and Mr. Jeffers was heading their way!

- **Has Mr. Jeffers found out about Jason and Max's investigation? Turn to page 72 to find out.**

At the same time, Jason and Max belted out the loudest screams they could manage.

Busby clamped his hands over their mouths, but it was too late.

"Who's in there?" someone called. "Gene, are you okay? It's me, Fred."

"Drat!" said Gene in a low voice. "It's Fred, the security guy!"

Security guy! Jason and Max's eyes got wide.

"What's he doing here?" Busby whispered.

"He makes his rounds every evening about now. He knows I work late so he stops by and we hang out sometimes." Gene looked embarrassed.

Busby stared at him. "Let me get this straight," he demanded. "You're working here to pull off a scam and you cozy up to the *security* guy?" He shook his head in disgust. "I don't believe this."

Gene got angry. "Just keep those two quiet and let me take care of this," he said in a huffy voice.

Gene switched on the radio, turning the volume up to cover the muffled sound of the boys trying to talk with Busby's hand over their mouths. Then he put the messenger-style bag he always carried on his shoulder and walked over to the door.

He pulled it open it just a crack. "Hey, Fred," said Gene in his fake nasally voice. "Good to see you. I was just leaving. I'll walk with you on your way up the hill, okay?" Gene tried to slip through and pull up the door behind him, but Fred the Security Guy stopped the door with his hand.

"Wait a minute. I thought I heard you having some trouble in there," Fred said, trying to look into the office over Gene's shoulder. "Sounded like somebody screaming."

Gene laughed nervously. "What? Oh, that. That was just some rock song that came on the radio. You know those heavy metal guys—all that yelling's murder on the ears."

There was a long pause. Jason and Max strained against Busby, but he only gripped them tighter.

Finally Fred said, "Oh. Okay, then."

The boys could see Gene's relieved smile. They slumped with disappointment as he stepped outside with the security guard and started to pull up the door.

But at the last minute, Fred's hand shot out and pushed the door open. He muscled his way past a startled Gene into the office. Then he blinked in shock when he spotted the boys tied up on the floor and Busby crouched beside them with his hands fastened over their mouths.

"What in the world—" Fred the Security Guy started.

"Run!" Gene shouted.

Busby charged at Fred, knocking him to the floor. Then he raced out the door behind his partner.

"Go, go! You gotta catch them," Jason shouted to Fred.

The security guard clearly didn't know what was going on, but he scrambled to his feet and chased after the two criminals.

By the time Jason and Max were able to wiggle their way out of their ropes and race to the front of the park, Gene and Busby had been captured.

Fred had stayed on their trail, calling on his walkie-talkie for back up. He'd tackled Busby midway through the park, and another security guy had caught up with Gene farther ahead. Mr. Jeffers had been called and now the two men were handcuffed in the back of a security cruiser, waiting for the city police to arrive.

Jason and Max plopped down on a bench, trying to catch their breath.

"Look at them," Max said. "They're gonna be going away for a long time, don't you think?"

Jason nodded. "Yeah. Guess crime really doesn't pay!"

THE END

"Jason, we couldn't be any more innocent!" Max said, "It doesn't matter if he thinks we did any of it, dude."

"You're right," Jason agreed.

"I know I am. Let's just see what he wants so he'll get off our trail. Then we can get back on The Creep's trail," Max said.

"Hey kids!" the guy with the belly yelled. "Come back here. I need to talk to you."

The boys turned to face their follower.

"Yeah? What is it?" Jason asked.

"My name is Sergeant Steve Zigler," the guy said. "I have reason to believe that *you* two might be responsible for all the trouble at the park."

"What reason do you have?" Max asked defensively.

"Well, young man, there's been a lot of funny business going on and every time I checked into it, I saw you and your friend here hiding nearby."

This was just what Jason was afraid of!

"You boys are going to have to come with me. We're going downtown to headquarters," Zigler said.

. . . .

"I don't mean to be rude, Sergeant," Max spoke up, "but we haven't done anything wrong. Besides, where is your badge? Shouldn't you show us your badge?"

"Um. Well," the sergeant seemed to be confused. "That's just a TV thing, showing you the badge. Now listen to me, I saw you at each of the rides, and I'm taking you to the police station!"

This sounded a bit suspicious to Jason and Max. Jason said, "I'd feel better if you just showed us the badge. How do we know you're a cop?"

Zigler was getting angrier. "I left the stupid badge in the cruiser, all right? Now just come with me—*now!*"

That was it for Jason and Max. There was no way this guy was a real cop. They took off, running away from him.

"Let's go to the Hedge Maze. He'll get lost in there for sure!" Jason yelled. They headed for the maze. When Max looked back, the guy was talking on his cell phone as he chased them.

"Howie! They're getting away," they heard Zigler

yell into the phone. "We're coming up on the log-flume ride. Come help me!"

As they passed the log-flume, Jason and Max saw The Creep heading toward them!

The Creep yelled at Zigler, "We're so close to finishing this thing! One more day, and we'll own this park and live like kings!"

"I hope you're right, Howie!" Zigler yelled back.

Jason and Max led Zigler and Howie into the Hedge Maze. The two boys knew exactly how to get from the front of the maze to the end and did so with no problem. The two goons, however, had gotten hopelessly lost.

"I'm sure they'll be stuck in there for a while," Jason said to Max. "But you stay here and guard the exit. I'll get my dad."

Jason ran off to find Mr. Jeffers. Max sat at the exit and listened to Zigler and Howie try to find their way out.

"Where in the world are we?" Howie asked.

"We're in some sort of plant labyrinth," Zigler answered.

"Very good, Mr. Smarty Clown," Howie said. "I know that, but how do we get out?" He was really frantic now.

Max heard the two men arguing about their plan. They were sabotaging the park to run down its value. Then they were going to buy the park from its owners at a cheap price. This was something Howie kept referring to as a "Do-It-Yourself Discount."

When Jason and Mr. Jeffers arrived at the maze a while later, Howie and Zigler were still at it trying to find their way out. And they would be trapped for a long time after that, too—behind steel bars in jail!

THE END

"We should start with the pen," Jason said again. "I can get a list of the employees at Volcania, and then we can find this EXB and pay him a visit! How many people can there be with an *X* for a middle initial?"

"Fine; let's go," Max backed down. "I'll keep the drill in case we need it later." He stuffed it in his backpack.

They headed over to the main office, discussing how they'd get information from EXB when they found him. "We could just ask him about the pen," Max suggested. "Get right to it."

"No way, man," Jason replied. "We shouldn't tip him off that we know anything. That's our edge. Right, Busby?"

Busby nodded. "Right."

They reached the office and Jason did the talking.

"Hi, Jason," said Dora Lee, the receptionist. "How's it going?"

"Great!" Jason replied. "It's just that we found this company pen a little while ago and wanted to return it to the owner. Do you have a list of employees we could look at to find out who it belongs to?"

"Sure thing," said Dora. She rummaged around until she found a company phone directory. She handed him the list. "That's really nice of you, Jason," she said as she picked up the ringing telephone.

The three huddled around the directory, looking for EXB. "I found it!" said Max. "It's right there between Mr. Ely Yonkers Bon and Ezra Sean Boreing—Ernestine Xena Bonds!"

"A woman!" Busby gasped.

"I don't think I know her," Jason said. "What department does she work in?"

"Kiddie coaster design," Max answered.

"Well, let's go talk with Ernestine Bonds and find out if she has a reason to sabotage the park," Busby said.

So they walked to the design building, found Ernestine's office, and knocked on her door. Jason was surprised when she opened the door—she reminded him of his grandmother! She was a sweet-looking old lady who wore a flowery dress and sensible shoes. Her office was full of cute porcelain frogs of all sizes. She didn't fit the description of any criminal, that was for sure. Jason introduced himself and told her who his father was.

"Oh, how nice," she said. "Your father is such a wonderful man."

"Thanks." Jason then proceeded to tell the story they had made up on their way. "Since Max and I spend every day here, my dad decided that we should start learning a bit about the park. We are doing employee satisfaction surveys," Jason lied. "And this is Larry Busby. He's here to supervise our work."

"Okay," Ernestine said. "Anything for Mr. Jeffers!"

Talking to her, all they learned was how much she loved coming to work and how much she hated riding roller coasters. She told them about her latest design, a mini-coaster she called LadyBug. "It's for the little ones who are too afraid to ride the big coasters—like my grandchildren. And me!"

"How long have you worked here, ma'am?" Max asked politely.

"I just celebrated my five-year anniversary with Volcania!" she answered.

"Wow. Congratulations. Did you get a cool pen with your initials on it?" Jason asked. "My dad got one when he hit the big five."

"Yes, I did! I loved that pen, but I lost it just the other day," Ernestine replied. "The last time I remember having it was when we were checking out a patch of land near Lava Lake. We're looking for a place to build LadyBug, you see. I must have dropped it then."

It didn't sound to Max like she could be responsible for *anything* mean, let alone sabotaging an amusement park. He was itching to move on to the drill and said, "I think that's all we need, Mrs. Bonds. Thanks so much for helping us!"

Jason had a few more questions to ask, but Max was hustling him out of the office. He reluctantly agreed. "Yes, thank you."

The three investigators left her office. "She's so

obviously innocent," Max said. "No way she'd do anything like this. She's too sweet!"

"I know, but there's something about her that bothers me," Jason said. "Maybe I could have gotten to it if you hadn't ended our conversation!"

"It's a dead end, Jase," Max answered. "Give it up."

"Hey, don't forget where we found that pen," Busby chimed in. "If you ask me, she was a bit *too* nice. Sweet little ol' ladies can be deceiving. You haven't met my mother!"

- Do Jason, Max, and Busby keep investigating Ernestine? Turn to page 52.

- Or do they move on and investigate the drill? Turn to page 100.

Jason and Max stood there, facing their former friend. Gene approached them with a toothy grin.

It was as if Gene had turned into a totally different person! But Jason tried his best to get through to him. "Gene, wait! It's *us*, Jason and Max. We're your friends, remember?"

"Shut up!" Gene snarled.

"But why are you doing this? What are you doing?" Jason asked.

"Yeah, Gene," Max jumped in. "You were the greatest designer ever! You still are. Why are you ruining it?" Max was not only really scared, but he was also upset that his idol had turned out to be such a jerk!

"That's just it," Gene explained. "I'm not the greatest designer, and I never have been. I just steal an idea from a designer here and add that to a great design there. Do that and, pretty soon, you have a killer ride like the Dragon Fly."

Gene shook his head sadly. "Only none of it was mine. I wanted to stop it, really. I mean, I felt guilty and I knew sooner or later I'd get caught. So

I decided to get out after one big score that would provide me with all the money I'll ever need!"

"How would ruining the rides make you money?" Jason asked.

"It was to distract the other engineers so I could copy all their files. You can make a lot of money selling that information," Gene confessed. "I can't believe I..." He was so upset he couldn't even finish his sentence.

Jason saw a tear fall from Gene's eye. They were actually talking him down! Boy, is Dad going to be glad when Max and I hand over Gene and save his job, Jason thought.

But Gene's eyes quickly dried up. "But I can't let myself get caught now!" he said frantically.

He ran to his desk, opened a drawer, and pulled something out. He walked toward Jason and Max with his hands behind his back. He let out a horrible cackle, then pulled a rope from behind his back. He started swinging it in the air like a cowboy with his lasso.

He threw the loop around Jason and Max and

pulled. Jason and Max were suddenly smooshed together back-to-back. The rope was tightly wound around their waists, but they could still move their legs and arms. Bracing against Jason, Max jumped up and kicked Gene. Gene flew into the air and landed right into the Dragon Fly model coaster.

The model crumbled with the impact, and Gene was completely covered by the twisted track.

"Let's get out of here!" Max yelled as he loosened the rope and freed Jason and himself.

"Dude, you are such a ninja! Did you see how he flew?" Jason was impressed.

They ran out the basement door that led directly outdoors. As soon as they made it out, they saw a familiar face.

"Hey there, you two! It's me, Busby. How's the investigation going?" It was Larry Busby, the investigative reporter they'd met earlier by Lava Lake.

Jason was so wound up by the fight they'd just had, he could hardly answer. "Guy…basement… sabotage…tied up…"

Max tried and could only come up with "Um, er. Uh. What he said."

"Just calm down, take a deep breath, and tell me what happened," Busby said.

Jason pulled himself together and explained the whole story to Busby. He really loved telling the part where Max kicked Gene into the model of Dragon Fly. "And he's still down there!" Jason finished. "We've gotta get help. We should call the cops."

"No," Busby said excitedly. "We can't take the chance that he'll get away while we're calling the cops. We've got to go back in and take him down! The three of us can definitely handle him." Busby was really pumped up.

Max shook his head. "Busby, you didn't see the look in Gene's eyes when he was playing cowboy with his rope," he protested loudly. "He's totally lost it! I'm not going back in there. No way. Right, Jason?"

Busby interrupted before Jason could respond. "Do you want him to get away after everything he did to Volcania?" Busby demanded. "If he takes off with company secrets, your dad can kiss his job good-bye!"

- Do the three go back and take on Gene Patt? If so, turn to page 49.

- Or do they go call the police and let them handle Gene? If so, turn to page 91.